Elmo Gets Homesick

By Tish Sommers Rabe
Illustrated by Tom Brannon

A GOLDEN BOOK • NEW YORK

Published by Golden Books Publishing Company, Inc., in cooperation with Children's Television Workshop

 Library of Congress Catalog Card Number: 88-51202 ISBN: 0-307-29011-5 MCMXCVII

Daddy

"Where are we going?" Elmo asked his mommy as she packed his suitcase.

"Daddy is going with me on a business trip," said Mommy, "and Daisy is going to camp, and you're going to visit Grandma and Grandpa."

"Oh, that's right!" Elmo said happily.

He'd forgotten, just for a minute.

"You're a lucky monster," Daisy told Elmo. "You get to visit Grandma and Grandpa all by yourself."

"I can't wait!" said Elmo.

Daddy, Mommy, Daisy, and Elmo piled into the car and drove off to Grandma and Grandpa's house. Elmo counted all the red cars they passed, and Daisy counted all the blue ones.

When the car drove up, Grandma and Grandpa rushed out to greet them.

"We're so glad to see you!" they called.

"Where is my little Elmo?" asked Grandpa.

"Here I am!" yelled Elmo.

Grandpa gave him a big hug.

Soon it was time for Mommy, Daddy, and Daisy to leave. Daddy and Mommy kissed Elmo good-bye.

"You be a good little monster," said Mommy. "We'll see you soon."

Daisy hugged Elmo good-bye, too.

Elmo waved and waved until the car was just a tiny speck in the distance.

"Good-bye!" he called softly.

He had a shaky feeling in his tummy.

"Elmo dear," said Grandma, "I'm making a batch of monster marshmallow cookies and I need some help."

"OK," said Elmo.

He loved helping Grandma make cookies, and marshmallow cookies were his favorite.

Elmo ate four monster cookies and drank a glass of milk.

Then he and Grandpa talked about all the things they would do together during Elmo's visit. They even made a list of Elmo's favorite things.

After dinner it was time for Elmo to go to bed. He always stayed in the room with a window that looked out on Grandpa's apple tree. Elmo put on his pajamas and brushed his teeth.

Grandma tucked him in and sang Elmo his favorite song, "Mary Had a Little Monster."

"Good night, little Elmo," said Grandma, giving him a kiss.

"Good night, Grandma," said Elmo.

And he fell sound asleep.

The next morning Elmo woke up to the sound of a little bird singing in the apple tree. For a moment he didn't know where he was! He wasn't in his own bed at home on Sesame Street.

"Good morning, sleepy monster!" Grandpa said as he came into Elmo's room and sat on the bed. "It's a beautiful day. Let's get busy."

But Elmo didn't feel like getting busy.

"What's the matter?" Grandpa asked gently.

"I miss Mommy and Daddy and Daisy," Elmo said, "and my own room and Big Bird and Barkley and all my friends." Elmo began to cry.

“It sounds like you’re a little homesick,” Grandpa told him. “But I’ll tell you a secret.”

“What?” asked Elmo.

“When your daddy was a little monster, he used to get homesick, too.”

“He did?” asked Elmo.

“You’ll be seeing your mommy and daddy and Daisy and all your friends soon,” Grandpa reminded him, “and you’ll have lots to tell them about your visit.”

Elmo smiled.

“Come on,” said Grandpa, “let’s get busy doing those things on your list!”

So Grandma, Grandpa, and Elmo spent the next few days doing the things on Elmo's list.

They went apple picking in an orchard, and Grandma baked an apple pie when they got home.

"Wait until I tell Cookie Monster about Grandma's homemade apple pie!" said Elmo.

They visited a family of kittens.

"Oh," said Elmo, "Herry Monster loves kittens. I will tell him all about them when I get home."

Elmo took his first ride on a pony.
"Boy," he said, "if Daisy could only see me now."

And he taught Grandpa how to play Monster Marble Maze.

"Gee, Grandpa," said Elmo, "when I play with Bert, he always loses his marbles."

One day Grandpa showed Elmo the family picture album.

"Who is that?" asked Elmo.

"That's your great-grandfather Selmo," Grandpa said. "He was an opera singer with the Metropolitan Monster Opera when he grew up.

"And here's a picture of your daddy when he was just your age."

"Wow," said Elmo.

The next morning the doorbell rang.

"Are you Mr. Elmo Monster?" asked Patsy the mail carrier as she reached into her mailbag.

"Yes, I am," said Elmo.

"I have a postcard for you," said Patsy.

Elmo had never gotten his very own postcard before! Grandma read the postcard to him.

"'Dear Elmo,'" she read. "'We are having fun, but we miss our little Elmo. We'll see you soon. Love, Mommy and Daddy.'"

Grandpa had a postcard, too.

"Your mommy and daddy are coming to take you home tomorrow!" he told Elmo.

"Tomorrow!" Elmo gasped. "But we haven't done everything on my list!"

"I know," said Grandma. "You'll just have to come visit us again soon."

"I'm going to miss you," Elmo told Grandma and Grandpa the next morning, when his parents were coming to get him.

"We'll miss you, too," said Grandma.

Then Elmo said, "I can't wait to tell everybody on Sesame Street about all the things we did together!"

CRAYONS